NURSERY SONGS

THIRTY OLD-TIME
NURSERY SONGS
ARRANGED BY
JOSEPH MOORAT
& PICTURED BY
PAUL WOODROFFE

THE METROPOLITAN MUSEUM OF ART
AND THAMES & HUDSON NEW YORK

Nursery Songs was first published in 1912 by T. C. & E. C. Jack, London, and Frederick A. Stokes, New York.

This new edition of the book has been produced directly from the original watercolor illustrations, musical notations, and hand-lettered texts in the collection of The Metropolitan Museum of Art, New York.

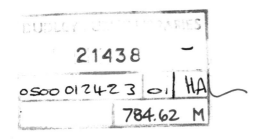

Published in 1980 by The Metropolitan Museum of Art
Thames and Hudson

Printed in Japan
ISBN 0-87099-242-2 (MMA)
ISBN 0-500-01242-3 (TH)

LIBRARY OF CONGRESS CATALOGING IN PUBLICATION DATA

Moorat, Joseph, ed.
　Thirty old-time nursery songs.

　Reprint of the 1912 ed. published by T. C. & E. C. Jack, London, and F. A. Stokes, New York.
　SUMMARY: An illustrated collection of 30 familiar nursery songs including "Three Blind Mice," "Yankee Doodle," and "Ding Dong Bell."
　1. Children's songs. 2. Nursery schools—Music. 3. Kindergarten—Music. 4. Nursery rhymes. [1. Songs. 2. Folk songs. 3. Nursery rhymes] I. Woodroffe, Paul. II. Title.

M1990.M84T5　　1980　　784.6'2406　　80-16025

PREFACE

THIS book of old-time Mother Goose songs, first published in 1912, continued to delight the nursery world through the 1920s. Most families knew all thirty rhymes by heart, everyone had his or her particular favorite, and half the pleasure of choosing which one to sing next was to keep the pages turning and to revel in the wonderful illustrations.

Even when the fun of singing, dancing, or acting out the songs was over and the book closed, there was still the cover to marvel at time and again. How many children found the black cat dressed in pink and playing the fiddle so irresistible that they snuck the book off the piano, scurried upstairs to bed with it, and hid it under the pillow?

The illustrations for *Nursery Songs* were made between 1906 and 1907, though the book was not published by T. C. & E. C. Jack in London and Frederick A. Stokes in New York until 1912. The artist who decorated these pages with such delicacy and humor was Paul Vincent Woodroffe. Born in India in 1875, he spent his childhood in Bath, England. After studying at Stonyhurst College and London's Slade School of Art, he became a typographer and illustrator, specializing in bookplates, nursery rhymes, songs, and poems. This volume was his third in collaboration with Joseph Moorat, who arranged the songs, but it was the first to be printed in color. It is also the best known of the eight books Woodroffe illustrated. The artist's other works include *Songs from Shakespeare's Plays* (1898) and *Aucassin and Nicolette* (1902). Woodroffe, who was strongly influenced by Walter Crane, Laurence Housman, and the Art Nouveau movement, is also known for his stained glass, especially the windows depicting the Mysteries of the Rosary in the Lady Chapel of New York's Saint Patrick's Cathedral.

These songs and illustrations have lost none of their appeal in the last half-century, and it would be hard to think of anything that would have pleased the artist more than to know that parents and children again have the chance of delighting in the book he had such a wonderful time illustrating.

BRYAN HOLME

LIST OF SONGS

DAME GET UP 1	LOOBY LOO 17
OLD KING COLE 2	THE FAIRY SHIP 18
GIRLS AND BOYS COME OUT TO PLAY 4	I HAD A LITTLE NUT-TREE . . 19
THE JOLLY TESTER 5	OVER THE HILLS AND FAR AWAY 20
OH, WHAT HAVE YOU GOT FOR DINNER MRS. BOND? . . . 6	SWEET LAVENDER 21
HEY DIDDLE DIDDLE 7	THE PLOUGHBOY 22
JACK AND JILL 8	POOR MARY SITS A-WEEPING . 23
HUMPTY DUMPTY 9	GOOD KING ARTHUR 24
SING A SONG OF SIXPENCE . . 10	THREE BLIND MICE 25
HERE WE GO ROUND THE MULBERRY BUSH 11	A FOX WENT OUT 26
THE FROG AND THE CROW . . 12	WHAT ARE LITTLE BOYS MADE OF? 28
LITTLE BO-PEEP 14	YANKEE DOODLE 29
TOM, TOM THE PIPER'S SON . . 15	I SAW THREE SHIPS 30
DING DONG BELL 16	BAA! BAA! BLACK SHEEP . . 31
	THE JOLLY MILLER 32
	HUSH-A-BYE BABY 33

DAME, GET UP

Dame, get up & bake your pies, bake your pies, bake your pies,

Dame, get up & bake your pies, On Christmas day in the morning.

2 Dame, what makes your maidens lie? &c

3 Dame, what makes your ducks to die? &c

4 Their wings are cut, they cannot fly, &c

OLD KING COLE

fiddles

p. Moderato

p

Old King Cole was a mer·ry old soul, And a

cres

mer·ry old soul was he: He called for his pipe, and he

called for his bowl, And he called for his fid·dlers three. Now

cres

ev·ery fid·dler had a fid·dle, And a ve·ry fine fid·dle had

he. Twee · dle - dee, twee · dle - dee, went the fid · dler's three, With King
O there's none so rare as can com · pare,

Cole and his fid · dlers three.

GIRLS & BOYS COME OUT TO PLAY

mf. brightly

Girls & boys come out to play The moon doth shine as bright as day;

Leave your sup·per, & leave your sleep, & come to your play·fel·lows in the street;

Come with a whoop, & come with a call, Come with a good will or not at all.

Up the lad·der & down the wall, A half·pen·ny roll will serve you all.

THE JOLLY TESTER

I love six·pence, pret·ty lit·tle 6·pence, I love 6·pence bet·ter than my life,

I spent a pen·ny of it, I lent a·no·ther, And I took 4 pence home to my wife.

2   O my little fourpence, pretty little fourpence,
       I love fourpence better than my life;
    I spent a penny of it, I lent another,
       And I took twopence home to my wife.

3   O my little tuppence, pretty little tuppence,
       I love tuppence better than my life;
    I spent a penny of it, and I lent the other,
       And I took nothing home to my wife.

4   O my little nothing, my pretty little nothing,
       What will nothing buy for my wife?
    I have nothing, I spend nothing;
       I love nothing better than my wife.

OH, WHAT HAVE YOU GOT FOR DINNER, MRS BOND?

Moderato

"Oh, what have you got for din·ner, Mrs. Bond?" "There's

2nd John Ost·ler, go fetch me a duck·ling or two, John

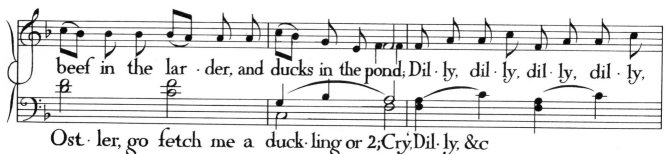

beef in the lar·der, and ducks in the pond, Dil·ly, dil·ly, dil·ly, dil·ly,

Ost·ler, go fetch me a duck·ling or 2; Cry, Dil·ly, &c

come to be killed, For you must be stuffed, and my cus·to·mers filled"

"I've been to the ducks that are swimming in the pond,
    And they won't come no how to the killing, Mrs. Bond;
I cried 'dilly, dilly, dilly, dilly, come' "&c.

Mrs. Bond went down to the pond in a rage,
    With plenty of onions and plenty of sage;
She cried, "Come, you little wretches, come, and be killed,
    For you shall be stuffed, and my customers filled!"

6

HEY DIDDLE DIDDLE

p Allegretto

Hey did·dle, did·dle, The cat and the fid·dle, The cow jumped o·ver the

moon, The lit·tle dog laughed to see such sport & the dish ran a·way with the spoon.

JACK & JILL

V.1 Jack and Jill went up the hill, To fetch a pail of wa·ter,
V.3 Jill came in and she did grin, To see Jack's pa·per plas·ter,

End here finally.

Jack fell down and broke his crown, And Jill came tum·bling af·ter.
Mo·ther vexed did whip her next, For caus·ing Jack's dis·as·ter.

V.2 Up Jack got and home did trot, As fast as he could ca·per,

Went to bed to mend his head, With vin·e·gar and brown pa·per.

HUMPTY DUMPTY

Moderato

Humpty Dumpty sat on a wall, Humpty Dumpty had a great fall; All the King's horses, And all the King's men, couldn't put poor Humpty Dumpty together again.

SING A SONG of SIXPENCE

mf

Sing a song of six·pence, a poc·ket full of rye;

Four & twen·ty black·birds baked in a pie; When the pie was o·pen the

birds be·gan to sing, Was·n't that a dain·ty dish to set be·fore the King

The King was in his counting-house counting out his money;
The Queen was in the parlour eating bread and honey;
The maid was in the garden hanging out the clothes,
There came a little dicky-bird, and pecked off her nose.

HERE WE GO ROUND
THE MULBERRY BUSH

mf. brightly

Here we go round the mulberry bush, Here we go round the mul·berry bush,

End here finally.

Here we go round the mul·berry bush on a fine fros·ty mor·ning.

p

This is the way we *wash our hands, This is the way we wash our hands,

This is the way we wash our hands on a fine fros·ty mor·ning.

mf

*In succeeding verses sing 'dry our hands,' ~ 'clap our hands, ~ 'warm our hands.'

THE FROG & THE CROW

p. Allegretto

A jol·ly fat frog lived in the ri· ver swim, O! A

come·ly black crow lived on the ri· ver brim, O! "Come on

shore, come on shore," said the crow to the frog, and then, O! "No, you'll

bite me, No, you'll bite me," Said the frog to the crow a·gain, O!

2   "O! there is sweet Music on yonder green hill, O!
            And you shall be a dancer, a dancer in yellow,
        All in yellow, all in yellow." said the crow to the frog, & then O!
        "All in yellow, all in yellow." said the frog to the crow again, O!

3   "Farewell, ye little fishes, that in the river swim; O!
            I go to be a dancer, a dancer in yellow."
      "O beware! O beware!" said the fish to the frog, & then O!
      "I'll take care, I'll take care." said the frog to the fish again, O!

4   The frog began a swimming, a swimming to land, O!
          The crow began a hopping to give him his hand, O!
      "Sir, you're welcome, Sir, you're welcome." said the crow * to the frog & then O!
      "Sir, I thank you, Sir, I thank you," said the frog to the crow again, O!

5   "But where is the music on yonder green hill, O?
         And where are all the dancers, the dancers in yellow?
      All in yellow, all in yellow?" said the frog to the crow, & then O!
      But he chuckled, O! he chuckled, & ~ then O!! ~ & ~ then O!!!

& that was the sad end of the frog

LITTLE BO-PEEP

Little Bo-Peep has lost her sheep, And can not tell where to find them; Let them alone, and they'll come home, & bring their tails behind them

2

Little Bo-Peep fell fast asleep,
  And dreamt she heard them bleating;
But when she awoke, she found it a joke,
  For they were still a-fleeting.

3

Then up she took her little crook,
  Determined for to find them,
She found them indeed, but it made
    her heart bleed,
  For they'd left their tails behind 'em.

4

It happened one day, as Bo-Peep did stray
  Into a meadow hard by,
There she espied their tails side by side,
  All hung on a tree to dry.

5

She heaved a sigh and wiped her eye,
  Then went o'er hill and dale-o,
And did what she could, as a shep-
    herdess should,
  To tack to each sheep its tail-o!

TOM, TOM THE PIPER'S SON

Brightly

Tom, Tom, the pi·per's son, Stole a pig and a·way did run; The

pig was eat, and Tom was beat, And Tom went howl·ing down the street.

DING DONG BELL!

Ding dong bell! Pus·sy's in the well! Who put her in?

Lit·tle Tom·my Lin. Who pulled her out? Lit·tle Tom·my Stout. What a

naugh·ty boy was that To drown poor pus·sy ~ cat, Who

ne'er did an·y harm, But killed all the mice in fa·ther's barn

LOOBY LOO

Here we go loo·by loo, Here we go loo·by light, Here we go loo·by loo,

All on a Sa·tur·day night. All your right hands in, All your right hands out,

shake them a lit·tle, a lit·tle, And turn your·selves a·bout.

2. All your left hands in, &c, &c.

3. All your right feet in, &c, &c.

4. All your left feet in, All, &c, &c.

THE FAIRY SHIP

p moderato

I saw a ship a-sail-ing, A-sail-ing on the sea,…. And oh! it was a-

la-den with pret-ty things for me; There were com-fits in the ca-bin, And apples in the

rall

hold; The sails were made of sa~tin, And the mast was made of gold.

The four-and-twenty sailors
That stood between the decks,
Were four-and-twenty white mice
With rings about their necks.

The captain was a duck, a duck,
With a jacket on his back,
And when the fairy ship set sail,
The captain he said, "Quack!"

I HAD A LITTLE NUT-TREE

p. moderato

I had a lit·tle nut tree, no·thing would it bear,

But a sil·ver nut·meg, and a gold·en pear; The King of Spain's daughter

came to vi·sit me And all for the sake of my lit·tle nut tree.

P   W

OVER the HILLS and FAR AWAY

p. brightly

Tom he was a pi · per's son, He learnt to play when
Tom with his pipe he made such a noise, That he pleased both

he was young; But all the tunes that he could play, Was
girls and boys, And they stopped to hear him play,

"O · ver the hills and far a · way, O · ver the hills and a

great way off, The wind shall blow my top knot off."

SWEET LAVENDER

p. brightly

1st V. La·ven·der's blue, did·dle, did·dle! La·ven·der's green; When I am
3rd V. Some to make hay, did·dle, did·dle! Some to cut corn; Whilst you and

King, did·dle, did·dle! You shall be Queen
I, did·dle, did·dle! Keep our·selves warm.

End ✱here

2nd Verse
Call up your men, did·dle, did·dle!

Set them to work — Some to the plough, did·dle, did·dle! Some to the cart.

P   W

THE PLOUGHBOY

Allegretto

My dad·dy is dead, but I can't tell you how; He left me six hor·ses to fol·low the plough; With a whim wham wad·dle ho! Strim stram strad·dle ho! Bub·ble ho! pret·ty boy o·ver the brow.

ritar

2. I sold my six horses to buy me a cow;
   And wasn't that a pretty thing to follow the plough?   With a whim,&c.
3. I sold my cow to buy me a calf;
   But I ne'er made a bargain but I lost the best half.   With a whim,&c.
4. I sold my calf to buy me a cat,
   To sit by my fire and warm her little back.   With a whim wham, &c.
5. I sold my cat to buy me a mouse,
   She took fire in her tail, and so burnt down my house. With a whim,&c

POOR MARY SITS A WEEPING

p. moderately slow

Poor Ma · ry sits a ~ weep · ing, a ~ weep · ing, a ~ weep · ing, Poor Ma · ry sits a ~ weep · ing, On a bright summer's day.

2
Pray Mary, what are you weeping for, A-weeping for, a-weeping for? ~ Pray ~ etc.

3
I'm weeping for a sweetheart, A sweetheart, a sweetheart. I'm weeping ~ etc.

4
Pray Mary, choose your lover, Your lover, your lover ~ Pray Mary, choose, etc.

GOOD KING ARTHUR

p. not too slow

When good King Ar-thur ruled this land, He was a good-ly King; He

stole three pecks of bar-ley meal To make a bag pud-ding

A bag pudding the Queen did make,
And stuffed it well with plums,
And in it put great lumps of fat —
As big as my two thumbs.

The King and Queen did eat thereof,
And noblemen beside,
And what they could not eat that night
The Queen next morning fried.

THREE BLIND MICE

p moderato

Three blind mice! See how they run! Three blind mice! See how they

mf. a little faster

run! They all run af·ter the far·mer's wife, Who cut off their tails with a

slower p

car·ving knife; Did you ev·er see such a sight in your life As three blind mice!

A FOX WENT OUT

p. moderato

A fox went out on a star·light night, And he
pray'd to the moon to give him some light, For he'd ma·ny miles to
go that night, Be·fore he could reach his den O! den O! den O! For
he'd ma·ny miles to go that night, Be·fore he could reach his den O!

2   He came at last to a farmer's yard,
        Where the ducks and geese declared it hard,
    That their sleep should be broken & their rest be marr'd
        By a visit from Mr. Fox O!

3   He took the grey goose by the sleeve;
        Quoth he "Madam Goose, now, by your leave,
    I'll take you away without reprieve,
        And carry you off to my den O!

4   Old Mother Slipper Sloppers jumped out of bed,
        And out of the window she popped her head,
    "Run, John, run! the grey goose has gone,
        And the fox is off to his den O!

5   John ran up to the top o' the hill,
        And blew a blast both loud and shrill;
    Says the fox "That is very pretty music, still —
        I'd rather be home at my den O!

6   At last he got home to his snug den,
        To his seven little foxes, eight, nine, ten;
    Says he, "Just see, what I've brought with me,
        With its legs all dangling down O!

7   He sat him down with his hungry wife;
        They did very well without fork or knife;
    They ne'er ate a better gooze in all their life,
        And the little ones picked the bones O!

WHAT ARE LITTLE BOYS MADE OF?

Brightly

What are lit·tle boys made of? What are lit·tle boys made of?
What are lit·tle girls made of? What are lit·tle girls made of?

Frogs and snails and pup·py dogs'tails, That's what are lit·tle boys made of.
Su·gar and spice and all that's nice, That's what are lit·tle girls made of.

3 What are young men made of?
      What are young men made of?
   Sighs and leers, and crocodile tears
      That's what our young men are made of.

4 What are young women made of?
      What are young women made of?
   Ribbons and laces, and sweet pretty faces,
      That's what are young women made of.

YANKEE DOODLE

mf merrily

Yan·kee Doo·dle came to town, Up·on a lit·tle po~~ny, He
First he bought a por·ridge pot, And then he bought a la~~dle, And

stuck a fea·ther in his cap, And called it *Mac·ca·ro~~ni.*
then he trot·ted home a·gain, As fast as he was a~~ble.

Moderato

I saw three ships come sail·ing by, Come sail·ing by, sail·ing by, I saw three ships come sail·ing by, On Christ·mas Day in the mor·ning

And what do you think was in them then,
In them then, in them then,
And what do you think was in them then,
On Christmas Day in the morning?

Three pretty girls were in them then, In them then, in them then,
Three pretty girls were in them then,
On Christmas Day in the morning.

And one could whistle, & one could sing, The other play on the violin;
Such joy was there at my wedding,
On Christmas Day in the morning.

BAA! BAA! BLACK SHEEP

p. moderato

"Baa! Baa! Black sheep, have you an·y wool?" Aye, mar·ry, have I,

three bags full; One for my mas·ter, and one for my dame, But

none for the lit·tle boy that lives down the lane.

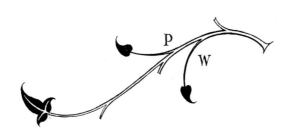

THE JOLLY MILLER

p. moderato

There was a jol·ly mil·ler once Lived on the ri·ver Dee; He

worked & sang from morn till night, No lark more blithe than

a little slower   *a tempo*

he.   And this the bur·den of his song For e·ver used to be, "I

care for no·bo·dy, no not I, And no·bo·dy cares for me."